The Adventures of Miss Myrtle

Enjoy

Nancy o Wyn

The Adventures of Miss Myrtle

NANCY AND WYN PRIOR

TATE PUBLISHING
AND ENTERPRISES, LLC

Published by Tate Publishing & Enterprises, LLC
127 E. Trade Center Terrace | Mustang, Oklahoma 73064 USA
1.888.361.9473 | www.tatepublishing.com

Tate Publishing is committed to excellence in the publishing industry. The company reflects the philosophy established by the founders, based on Psalm 68:11,
"The Lord gave the word and great was the company of those who published it."

Book design copyright © 2014 by Tate Publishing, LLC. All rights reserved.
Cover design by Gian Philipp Rufin
Interior design by Gram Telen

Published in the United States of America
ISBN: 978-1-63268-838-5
Juvenile / Animals / Turtles
14.07.03

This book is dedicated as a memorial and tribute to Miss Myrtle, a great little gal who adopted us and gave us great joy for several years. We miss you.

Preface

This little critter, a box turtle, came into our lives in the spring of 2008 when my wife, Nancy, found her upside down in the grass of our front yard next to some rockery around the flower beds. Nancy got her upright and gave her a saucer of water after which she was on her way. The next day was a repeat of the first, at which time Nancy introduced her to our backyard.

We have made our yard into a welcoming place for birds, mainly cardinals, blue jays, doves, and small wildlife (squirrels and the like), complete with fresh water and a bird feeder, both of which are in continual use. The neighborhood cats know our yard is off-limits, but strays have learned to come for a drink and then immediately leave;—don't tell Nancy that cats cannot be trained!

After a day a two, our cat, JJ, would be watching for Miss Myrtle at the backdoor, raise the alarm, and there we would find Miss Myrtle under the grille on our back patio, in the shade at about 8:00 a.m. every second or third day, waiting for food. After a short while, we became quite fond of her and started photographing her antics till she left and ambled off down the river rock around the house to the nearby Lantana or sago palm.

She leaves in late July each year for places unknown but returns in April to resume her antics as if she had never left.

Miss Myrtle passed away in July, 2012. What follows is our perception of what she may have been thinking as she enjoyed our backyard with all its various activities.

Enjoy the adventures of Miss Myrtle.

My Name Is Myrtle

Hi,

    My name is Myrtle, and I'm a pretty Texas gal!

    My name is spelled funny, but it sounds the same as turtle—because I am a box turtle.

I am about the size of a grown-up's hand, which is not very big for a wild animal.

What makes me special is that I have two shells. The top shell is brown, tall, and round, a bit like a football; the bottom shell is almost flat.

When I am out playing, I can stick my head out the front; my four short legs and feet reach the ground so that I can run.

I cannot move very fast because my legs are so short. I can run about as fast as a baby that has just learned to walk, which is not very fast.

When I get frightened or want to go to sleep, I can pull my head and legs inside my shells and close them both together so that nobody can see me.

In the winter time, I like to have a long sleep,—you humans call it hibernation,—where I find a safe place to sleep like under a big sago palm or under a lot of pine needles.

I make lots of friends with the other small animals, such as frogs, mice, and animals like that. I want you to meet my friend, Miss Fergie the frog. I think she's funny because she jumps everywhere. When she gets tired, she hides between pieces of wood on the side of the house.

I don't like cats and dogs because they are too big to play with. They want to use me like a football and that hurts.

When I see or hear them coming, I hide in my shell or under some pine needles or bushes.

I can hear dogs easily because they bark a lot, but cats are very quiet. They creep up slowly, and I do not hear them coming.

My Playground Has Gone

My forest has been taken away but not all the trees have gone.
Now there are houses for humans to live in with roads and fast cars. It is difficult for me to find a place to live and play. Where I used to play with my friends is now a house with a front yard with walls that I cannot climb.

Between the houses, the humans have planted grass. This is no fun because I can't play hide-go-seek with my buddies anymore, because a turtle cannot hide in grass.

This all happened when I was about ten years old.

Miss Myrtle and the Mountain

A few weeks ago, I went back to the place where I used to hide under the pine needles to sleep.

Now the humans have built a stone wall and put some flowers behind it. Flowers and stone walls are nice for the humans but a real problem for a small turtle. This wall is very small for humans but for a small turtle like me it looks like a…

…mountain

Now I cannot walk down my track to meet my friends. I must try and climb this wall.

The wall is a lot bigger than me, but let's give it a try.

…*oops!*

I fell over backwards, and now here I am with all four feet in the air and not able to move.

What shall I do now?

I can't stay like this for long; or I will die. Let me pull my head and feet inside my shell, close my shell, and then think what to do. Then I will not be afraid.

There's one of those humans passing by. Let me call out and see if she can hear me.

"Miss Nancy, please come over here and help me up!"

Wow! She has lifted me up and turned me the right way up,—let me peek outside my shell and see if she is a friendly person. She must be friendly; otherwise, she would not help me.

Miss Myrtle Meets Miss Nancy

Just my luck, it's Miss Nancy, and she is stroking the back of my shell and talking to me in a soft voice.

Ah! She has put me down in the grass and brought a saucer of water,—that is nice of her. I must remember to thank her for the drink.

That was a nice drink, but I think I will leave mountain climbing for another day.

Now she's picked me up again; I wonder what's going to happen now?

Miss Nancy is carrying me a long way and talking very fast to me in a funny language. I wonder what she is saying.

"Now, Miss Myrtle—"

How did she know my name? I wonder.

"—you just come with me to the backyard, and make that your home. You will be safe there with no cats or dogs in the yard. I send away all the strange cats that come in the yard. Here, there are no walls, just squirrels, woodpeckers, cardinals, blue jays, doves, pine needles, bushes to hide under, and plenty of water to splash around or to drink."

"Let me introduce you to Sir JJ. He's a Texas tabby cat that lives in our house. He never goes outside, so he will never be in the yard to hurt you."

Miss Nancy is wagging her finger at me, so I think I am getting a good telling off! Anyway, it sounds like a good arrangement to me. Let's see what this place is really like.

I Learn to Eat Lettuce

Miss Nancy has put me down on this stretch of flat grass. —That's okay, but everyone can see me, and I don't like that because cats and dogs can be dangerous for a small turtle. Let me go this way and explore a little bit, but first let's go and see if Miss Nancy is at the door and watching for me. I'll sit on the patio by this door and watch for her. These shoes are not in the way, but they sure make me feel small.

Oh, there she is now. Let me move out of here on to the patio in the open where she can see me.

"Hi, Miss Myrtle, are you ready for some breakfast now?"

I don't know what she is saying, but it sounds kind and gentle, so I will stay for a few minutes longer.

"Here you go, Miss Myrtle. Here is some lettuce for you to enjoy."

Wow, this is good stuff!

The inside pieces of this lettuce leaf are really tasty, but this outside stuff ,—*uggh!*—it's tough. I wonder, if I ask Miss Nancy nicely, if she will cut the leaf up a bit, so I can eat all the soft part first.

Ah yes, she has cut it up for me and this piece of soft lettuce leaf is a lot more tasty.

I Become a Pretty Lady

Now what is she doing? Miss Nancy has bent down and put a dab of red stuff on my shell. It doesn't hurt, and I can't see it, but I'm curious about it.

"Now, Miss Myrtle, I've put a very small dab of red nail polish on your shell, just like all young ladies put red nail varnish on their fingernails. This way, when you come by, I will always know that it is you, and I will give you breakfast!"

Good idea, Miss Nancy. That means that whenever I get hungry I can come by and get some more food. Sounds like a good idea to me,—thank you!

Now I have a full tummy, and my shell is all painted nice like the young ladies, so I think it is time to have a sleep. Perhaps I should find a nice warm cozy spot where I can rest safely through the winter until spring comes around.

All this moving about and climbing walls has really worn me out!

Good-bye, Miss Nancy, I need to have a sleep. I'll be back next year.

But let me think, *where should I go?* I know a good spot,— there is a sago palm just around the corner, and I have a pathway to it that goes under the fence. That should be ideal. Let me go and check that it hasn't been blocked to keep the stray cats and dogs out of the yard.

Miss Myrtle Meets Sir JJ, the Cat

That was a nice sleep that I had through a long cold winter. I found a good sleepy spot right under the sago palm with enough soft soil to bury down a little way and enough leaves and pine needles to keep me beautifully warm and well hidden.

Now I must walk round to the back of the house and see if I can attract Miss Nancy's attention. I'm really hungry after such a long sleep. But walking all the way to the back of the house will attract the attention of some cats, and I don't like them. I must hurry and be careful!

Here we are at the back patio. I'll just wait here a minute and perhaps Miss Nancy will see me.

Oh my goodness, I heard a cat's *meow!* I must hide,— where can I go? It's getting hot out here sitting in the Texas sun, so let me get in the shade under this object here. I've watched Miss Nancy cooking on the top of it, so she should soon come by.

This shade is nice, but I hope she sees me soon. I'm getting hungry.

Let me peek out.

There's that *meow* again!

Let me peek around this wheel at the door.

Oh, yes! The *meow* is coming from Sir JJ, the cat inside the house! I hope he is telling Miss Nancy that I am hungry and waiting here for my breakfast!

This looks promising. I can see Miss Nancy in the doorway. *Aha*! Here she comes!

"Good morning, Miss Myrtle. How are you today? Are you ready for breakfast yet?"

"Sir JJ, will you please keep quiet—you are sounding just like any other alley cat!"

"There, Miss Myrtle, that should keep him quiet for a little while, but you must learn to like Sir JJ. He lives with us inside the house. He never goes outside, and he watches at the door for you and lets me know when you arrive."

Myrtle Loves Bananas!

"Now, Miss Myrtle, I thought you might like to try some banana for a change. They are a bit softer than the lettuce, and it may be easier for you to chew. I'll put it under this grille, so you can stay in the shade."

Wow! How lucky can a little turtle get,—fresh bananas for breakfast—and carefully cut in half at that!

Oh, bother! I think these wretched flies also like the banana. This one is trying to steal some of my banana and landed on my nose,—it tickles!

I will just have to shake him off! That's better. Now I can enjoy my breakfast.

This is great, now I don't feel hungry anymore. I'll have to leave a little bit just to show Miss Nancy how grateful I am. Then I will have to find somewhere cool

where I can have a nap and sleep off all this breakfast. I must remember to come back tomorrow and see if she brings me breakfast again.

Maybe Sir JJ will keep a lookout for me. Perhaps I should change my mind about cats,— this one is being very helpful and alert. Best of all, he is in the house and can't hurt me!

Next Day–Miss Myrtle and the Strawberries

How lucky can a turtle get? The kitty has spotted me again, and I can hear him *meow* to Miss Nancy.

Here she comes.

"Good morning, Miss Myrtle, are you ready for breakfast yet? I don't have many bananas in the house, so I thought you would like to try some fresh strawberries with the banana for a change. They are a bit juicy and red, not white, but I think you will enjoy them.

Wow, these strawberries are delicious, and—oh, no,—I got some banana stuck on my face. And there's that pesky fly again.

He has his eye on my strawberries—I'll have to watch out for him. I guess he too knows that they are delicious and juicy.

Uh, oh! Here comes someone else who wants to try my strawberries and banana, but this one is a four-footed critter. I think she is called a gecko. With a name like that no wonder she can climb straight up and down the walls! I'll have to ask

Miss Nancy what she calls these little guys, and knowing Miss Nancy, she will have some funny name for them, but it won't be Myrtle—that's the name for turtles! I know what, I'll call her "Greta the Gecko"

"Hi there, Miss Greta!"

Oh dear, when she heard my voice she ran away. She must be a scaredy-gecko and not used to being around friendly turtles. Ah, there she is, just peeking around the corner of the house.

"Hi there, Miss Greta! How do you manage to climb straight up a wall? I want to find out, so that I can climb over the rocks in the front yard."

"I have very special feet that let me climb up steep walls and over glass. They are strong, so I can move very fast, and I can change color so I am well camouflaged," said Miss Greta,

"and I can hide in very small places where I can sleep in peace."

"That's not fair, Miss Greta, you seem to have all the advantages, even though you are only a small person."

"Don't you complain too much, Miss Myrtle…

…at least you have Miss Nancy bringing you food whenever you show up, nice soft bananas and those juicy strawberries. She doesn't bring me anything. I have to stay very, very still, clinging to glass all night in the dark, feeling very stupid, just hoping one of those flies will come near enough so that I can catch him with my tongue."

I guess I shouldn't complain too loud, at least I have plenty of food and water, and I don't have to catch it!

I feel a bit thirsty now after all that talking with Miss Greta. Let me go and find some water.

Miss Myrtle and the Squirrel

While I've been eating my banana and strawberries, I've been watching the birds and squirrels on the far side of the yard. I've seen some bright red cardinals with their babies. The babies look as big as their daddy who feeds them and fetches food for them. You can always recognize a Daddy cardinal by his bright red feathers. His babies always have a black beak, even while their feathers are grey as they grow up. If you watch closely you can see him put the seed in the baby cardinal's mouth. At least I don't have to do *that* with *my* babies!

One of his babies is sitting on the birdbath over there, looking as if he is getting impatient. I think I heard him call out,

"Hey, Daddy, what about me!"

I think Daddy cardinal makes them all take turns getting their food.

Mr. Woodpecker comes regularly, and when he arrives everyone else flies away. It must be that long beak of his. He collects a seed in his mouth and then just flies away. I think he must be feeding his babies somewhere nearby!

I've also seen a squirrel. I've talked to him before, and his name is Sydney. He is quite friendly and has a nice white tummy. He is eating the seed that has fallen down from the bird feeder.

"Hi there, Mr. Sydney, how are you today?"

"Hello, Miss Myrtle."

Mr. Sydney is a little bit rude. He never stopped eating as he said "Hello" and his mouth was full of food.

Just behind where the squirrel is eating his dinner is a round shiny thing. I don't know what it is, but I see the squirrels and the birds go there a lot. Let me watch for a few minutes and see what happens.

Just as I thought, Mr. Sydney goes there for a drink.

And there's a baby cardinal standing on the edge of the dish, wondering how to get a drink.

Here comes his dad. *Oh no!* Mr. Cardinal has jumped in the water. I guess he just wants to cool off by sitting in the water,

but no, he's decided to have a bath.

He is splashing away and has emptied all the water out of the dish!

Doesn't he know you should not have a bath in your drinking water?

And here's a baby woodpecker. He must be young because he's not sure what to do,—he's just looking at the water, and he is so tiny I can hardly see him.

Ah, ah, here comes Miss Dawn, the dove. They are very quiet and gentle birds, but she's on her own, so I wonder what her mate is doing. The doves are very gentle, so I know they will not bother me at all. They just pick up all the seeds that the squirrel and the woodpeckers leave, and they help to keep the yard tidy.

Oh dear! Here is that noisy blue jay, squawking all the time. Now the noisy blue jay arrives, and he jumps in the dish, splashes around, takes a bath, and empties all the water out of the dish!

Now nobody can get a drink!

Miss Myrtle Has a Bath

Now I will have to wait till the water turns on and fills the dish. Meanwhile, I will start to walk in that direction and watch for the water.

Aha! Here comes the water, drop by drop, so let me get to it before the blue jay arrives. This dish is deep, so I hope I can reach the bottom with my feet. Let me slide in slowly, —there we go,—oh, it is so nice and cool!

Aaaaaaah, let me just relax a while in this nice cool water and enjoy the scenery.

Oh dear, here comes Mr. Sydney, the squirrel. I wonder what he wants? I don't think there is enough room for the two of us. Does he want a drink? No! He has seen me and stopped. Maybe if I stare at him, he will go away and leave me alone in the water.

"Shoo, Mr. Squirrel"

There! He heard me shout at him, and he has turned and run away. Now I can enjoy my bath in peace.

That was a nice long bath, but now it's time to leave. So let me dry off, then go back and finish my breakfast.

Aha, here it is—just where I left it.

I've had a good day, now I want to go away, sleep, and have a good long rest. I'm tired out from all this swimming, and shouting at squirrels, and everything else. It's time for a long nap till next spring.

Let me say "Thank you" to Miss Nancy. Then she will remember to look for me next year.

"Hi there, Miss Nancy. Thank you for the banana and strawberries. See you next year."

"Bye, bye, Miss Myrtle. See you next year. Have a good sleep and stay safe. Bye, bye"

The End

Epilogue

July 19th, 2012 was a typical hot, humid and sultry July day in the Houston area. We had just returned from a trip into the city when we looked out of our kitchen window and saw Miss Myrtle very still, in a mulch area that we had never seen her visit before.

She was too still so we went outside, to find that she had died.

We make a point of giving any of God's creatures that die in our backyard a dignified burial with a silent prayer, so I started making preparations.

As she was laid to rest, there was an enormous loud clap of thunder like we rarely hear......and it suddenly started to rain very heavily.

And God cried for His child.

Note

Miss Myrtle was a wild animal, not our pet, therefore none of the photos are staged or planned; they were photographed as it happened. The photos were taken with a Canon G9™ camera with minor post processing.